Pirate the Seal

Acting on a sudden impulse, Ryan bent down and removed his shoes and socks then, rolling up his trousers, waded into the sea. Barks of approval exploded like loud laughter into the air. "Is that it? You want me to join you?"

Pirate was delighted, nodding his head and still barking. Ryan splashed back to the shore and rummaged in his school bag until he produced a pair of games shorts. As soon as he had changed into them, he rushed into the water and swam confidently to Pirate's side. At last the seal was quiet; he had achieved his goal. Ryan was in the sea with him: his domain.

Other Hippo Animal Stories:

Thunderfoot
Vanilla Fudge
Deborah van der Beek

A Foxcub Named Freedom
Brenda Jobling

Midnight Dancer
Midnight Dancer: To Catch a Thief
Midnight Dancer: Running Free
Midnight Dancer: Fireraisers
Elizabeth Lindsay

Animal Rescue
Bette Paul

Pirate the Seal

Brenda Jobling

Scholastic Children's Books,
Commonwealth House, 1–19 New Oxford Street,
London WC1A 1NU, UK
a division of Scholastic Ltd
London ~ New York ~ Toronto ~ Sydney ~ Auckland

First published by Scholastic Ltd, 1996

ISBN 0 590 13501 5

Typeset by TW Typesetting, Midsomer Norton, Avon

Printed by Cox & Wyman Ltd, Reading, Berks.

10 9 8 7 6 5 4 3 2 1

Dedicated to my mother, Jessie Beecher
and my daughter, Amy

Chapter 1

Eleven-year-old Ryan Thorpe closed the door to Lighthouse Cottage and stepped out into the morning mist hovering over the little island where he lived. It was cold, but the bright blue sky foretold of warmer weather later in the day.

Ryan set off along the path leading to the island school. It would take him ten minutes to walk there. To anyone living on the mainland, one room attached to the back of the island's little church would hardly constitute a school; to its ten pupils, all of different ages, it was the only school they had ever known. Miss Roberts, their teacher, worked hard, spending time with each one of them. Everyone had their own work assignment according to their age. Ryan was her oldest pupil and it was his greatest wish to move on to a large comprehensive school on the mainland later in the year.

As Ryan walked he could still taste the eggs he had hurriedly scrambled for breakfast, then eaten, as usual, alone. His father had been working since dawn. They seldom ate together. Ryan kicked a stone along the path and thought about the day ahead. The prospect of more time spent in the company of younger children filled him with despair. It wasn't that he disliked them – he often joined in their games, especially football – but he really needed a friend nearer his own age – someone out for some adventure; someone to take his mind off the gloomy atmosphere at home.

Ryan began to daydream. Perhaps he *would* go to that school on the mainland. It wouldn't be too long before he knew. His teacher was pleased with his work and had told him he had lots of ability. Life on the mainland to Ryan represented a wonderland of shops, sports centres, clubs and, most important of all, a place to meet children of his own age. At the island school, the children were too young. Out of school, he found the adults too old. As for home, he hardly ever saw his father.

Still deep in thought, Ryan turned a bend in the path, stumbled on the stone he had been kicking, and fell. "Ouch!" he exclaimed, clamping his hands over the graze which stung where little bits of grit had embedded themselves in the wound. "Ow, ow, *ow*!" he shouted as loud as he could. There was only the sea and sky to hear him and he was pleased for an excuse to vent the anger he bore his father.

Ryan's mother had died two years ago. He still missed her very much and often recalled the happy times they had spent before her illness. She smiled out of the photographs he kept in his room, with a warmth that Ryan could still conjure up. He found it hard to come to terms with spending the rest of his life without her, but he knew she would want him to enjoy life: think of her from time to time, but carry on and carve out a wonderful future, wherever he chose to live.

Matthew Thorpe, Ryan's father, had been devastated by the loss of his wife. It seemed as though he would carry his grief around for the rest of his days. He was solemn and had little time for Ryan. For Matthew, work was all that mattered. He could immerse himself in it, and, because he was good at it, he gained some satisfaction. For fourteen years he had been lighthouse keeper, taking the job shortly after he had married and fetching his young bride with him to live on the island. They were happy – and even happier with the arrival of Ryan. When the lighthouse was converted to automatic, Matthew was offered the job of island warden and allowed to remain in Lighthouse Cottage, where Ryan had been born. A familiar sight to the islanders, he rarely stopped to chat with them. But his lonely figure could often be seen striding the length of the island, ensuring that property and animals were safe. With head bowed, he challenged the winds that blew across the stark plateau of rock, twenty miles out to sea from the mainland.

Ryan sat on the ground, cleaning the dirt from his injured knee by spitting on to his hanky and rubbing it on the graze. He looked in the direction of school with disinterest. He was fed up and decided to give it a miss that morning. Instead of continuing along the path to school, he turned on to another path leading down to a cove he always regarded as special. It was sheltered on one side and Ryan liked to imagine that smugglers had once used it to land and hoard their goods. Carefully picking his way across the rocks, he spotted a place where he could sit in peace with just the sound of the waves lapping on to the shore, and the cry of seagulls for company. The mist had cleared enough to show a vague outline of the mainland.

Ryan felt in his bag for his sandwiches. He took them out and looked at them. They were squashed from his fall. His appetite instantly disappeared, so he tore at them, throwing the pieces to the gulls who swooped, gulping them down greedily in one swallow. Two seagulls swept in front of him, grabbing the same piece in their beaks, before they flew high into the air, both refusing to let go of the bread. High up, they battled, before the chunk fell to the shore, only to be hurriedly devoured by another seagull. When the gulls had eaten the last scrap of Ryan's lunch, they flew away to preen themselves on the cliffs. Ryan gazed casually around the cove until his attention was drawn to a rock pool nearby, where an old red Frisbee lay discarded; probably left behind by a holiday visitor. He picked it up and threw it out to sea, waiting for the waves to return it to the shore. He kept this up for about half an hour, feeling lonely.

Eventually he decided he might as well go to school; some company was better than none, even if it was tale-telling girls, or boys who had trouble kicking a football straight. Picking up his bag, he hurled the battered old Frisbee to the waves and moved off across the rocks. Ryan had hardly taken a few steps when, to his surprise, something hard hit him on the back of his head. It was the Frisbee. Angrily, he spun around – he thought he had been alone. All he saw was the sea, its waves endlessly slapping on to the shore. Once again he threw the object far out to sea, watching it land in the dark water. He looked around and, seeing nothing unusual, walked away. Again, the Frisbee whistled through the air, landing at his feet this time. Ryan snatched it up and, turning to confront the apparently deserted cove, shouted, "Come out! Show yourself!" But no voice replied. Instead a bark – a sort of croak – came from the waves. Ryan peered hard at the dark, green water until he found himself looking into two black, shining eyes set in a silky grey head. Their owner wore a comical smile on his young seal's face.

The seal bobbed up and down in the water, continuing to bark at Ryan, who began to laugh. He had seen many seals in the waters around the island. They could be quite friendly, but this one seemed especially eager to make his acquaintance. The young creature showed no fear of Ryan, and moved his inquisitive head from side to side, checking he had the boy's full attention. The seal began barking loudly, until Ryan realized that he might want the Frisbee back. He picked it up and hurled it out to sea. Skilfully, and with minimum effort, the seal calculated the speed of the flying object, raised his head from the water, and snatched it out of the air with his mouth. A swift flick of his head sent it flying back to Ryan, who was delighted.

"*So*, you want to *play*, do you?" he called to the seal. "I think you should know that around here, I'm regarded as pretty hot at this game."

But there was no contest. No matter how much Ryan sought to spin, flick, or skim the Frisbee past the seal, the creature caught it with ease every time. As for Ryan, the seal had him slipping about all over the rocks, trying desperately to catch the Frisbee before it landed. The seal enjoyed Ryan's antics immensely. Whenever Ryan missed a catch, he barked loudly, mocking the boy who was no match for him.

The two played happily, oblivious to anything but their game. After a while, Ryan paused for breath, exhausted from slipping about on the seaweed-covered rocks. He stood up and breathed in deeply. His cheeks tingled and sweat trickled down his neck. Glancing at his wristwatch, he panicked. School! He really ought to put in an appearance before lunchtime. Ryan looked at the young seal, who was anticipating the next throw, and yelled, half expecting a reply, "I'll see you later!" He threw the Frisbee and hurriedly slithered his way back over the rocks to the path.

The animal held the battered old toy in his mouth, staring after Ryan as he fled. Slightly bemused by Ryan's sudden departure, he nevertheless sensed the game to be only temporarily over and sank silently beneath the waves. Ryan stopped to look back when he reached the top of the path. There was no sign of the seal; it was as though he had never been there. But Ryan knew it was no day-dream: his cheeks still tingled and sweat dampened his forehead. Ryan was happy. A friend! At last, a friend! He longed to see the seal again and determined to visit the cove on his way home from school.

With a smile on his face, in elated mood, Ryan ran all the way to school, prepared to admit to his teacher that he had taken the morning off. His reason? He just didn't feel like attending. Ryan knew he would receive some form of punishment, like tidying the craft cupboard during his lunch break, and there would of course be a letter for his father, informing him of his son's absence. It did, after all, constitute bad behaviour. Ryan wasn't bothered about staying in through the lunch break but he didn't look forward to handing his father a letter to say he had skipped school that morning.

* * *

Throughout his lessons Ryan's thoughts often wandered to the seal. Miss Roberts told him to stop daydreaming. He had been recalling the animal's face and wanted to laugh out loud when he remembered the black mark around one eye, like a pirate's patch. Ryan decided that Pirate would be a good name for his new friend.

Just before the end of school that day, Miss Roberts called Ryan over to her desk. She was putting a note for his father into an envelope which she licked, then handed to her pupil. "I appreciate your honesty," she told him. "There are mornings when I don't feel like coming in to school either, but unless there is a very good reason for not attending, we just have to get on with it."

Miss Roberts watched him go. She liked the boy and imagined that life at home had been very difficult since his mother had died. She was aware that Ryan was probably very unhappy at times, sharing a home with his father who always looked so miserable.

With the note in his pocket, Ryan took off at full speed for the cove. He was out of breath when he arrived, eager to see the little grey head bobbing up and down like a fisherman's float in the waves. But there was no sign of the seal. Ryan decided to skim some flat pebbles across the surface of the water, in the hope of attracting him if he lurked below. After twenty minutes or so, the seal still hadn't appeared. The tide was beginning to rise and slowly creep its way up the shore. Disappointed, Ryan threw the pebbles left in his hand to the waves, and headed for home.

His father acted much as Ryan had anticipated when he opened the note from Miss Roberts. He looked briefly at Ryan, shook his head in a way that denoted disappointment, then let the note drop from his hands on to the table. Ryan felt a surge of anger within him and he blurted out, "*Say* something, Dad! Shout at me! Send me to my room, but don't just *ignore* me."

Matthew Thorpe watched with disinterest

as his son fled the room. Upstairs, Ryan sat on his bed with his legs drawn up to his chest and his arms wrapped around them. The view from the window showed an ocean of waves moving towards him, gradually calming and soothing the hurt he felt inside.

Next morning, he set off for school earlier than usual, intent on returning to the cove in the hope of seeing the seal again. He almost slid down the path to the rocks and, using his new name for the seal, shouted, "Pirate!" as loudly as he could manage, over and over again. He threw pebbles into the water, waved his arms about and made as much noise as possible in the hope of attracting the seal's attention – all without effect. The only response his performance managed to attract came from two seagulls who took to the air shrieking with annoyance at the antics of the boy on the shore.

Ryan decided it must have been luck that brought the seal to the cove the day before. The creature probably wouldn't appear there again. He shuffled off to school feeling sad. Halfway up the cove path he heard a noise and turned. To his delight, he saw the seal's proud head cruising above the surface of the water, the old Frisbee clenched firmly in his mouth. At first, Ryan was tempted to ignore him – he'd show the creature he wasn't desperate for the company of a seal! But Ryan couldn't hide his obvious pleasure at seeing him again. He jumped up and down, waving his arms and calling, "Ahoy, Pirate! I'm over *here*!"

The instant Ryan reached the water's edge, the Frisbee landed with a splash at his feet. He picked it up and hurled it high into the air above the seal, who caught it with ease and threw it straight back. Soon a frantic game of catch was underway. As Ryan slithered across the rocky shore to retrieve the Frisbee, he stumbled across his school bag, suddenly realizing how little time he had left to reach school. He was about to return the Frisbee to Pirate, then changed his mind. If he retained it after the game, it might ensure Pirate's

return to the cove. Ryan called to him to let him know he would be back after school. Pirate barked at first, then began to wail as Ryan ran off. In fact the noise he made was both loud and distressed.

"Pirate, what's the matter? I must go now – but I'll be back." The awful wailing continued. Ryan was concerned that the animal might be injured. "Are you hurt?" he enquired. He threw the Frisbee into the water to see whether Pirate could swim after it. The battered old ring flew towards the seal, who eagerly snatched it, clamped it between his jaws and swam contentedly on his way. Ryan laughed out loud at Pirate's tactics which ensured he got his own way; as far as the seal was concerned, the Frisbee belonged to him. Ryan continued to laugh as he bounded over the rocks to school, his mind full of his new friend.

Chapter 2

The sun's rays were still strong enough to warm the earth when school finished for the day. Ryan knew his father would be working at the other end of the island and probably wouldn't return until late evening. Grabbing his books, and almost knocking Miss Roberts off balance, he made a speedy exit from the classroom, stopping only when he reached the cove.

Miss Roberts had been intrigued that day to find Ryan spending both breaks, and his lunch hour, searching through the limited supply of books the school possessed. At one point, she had looked over his shoulder and noticed all the books were open on pages referring to seals. Ryan decided to tell her about Pirate and revealed his attempts to draw a seal, copying from photographs in the books. Cautiously checking that no one else could hear him, he whispered, "Please don't tell anyone about him. I would hate him to stop visiting me in the cove. He's not like any other seal – he doesn't just do tricks. Somehow, he seems to understand what I say to him. Even though we are such different animals, he communicates with me – like a real friend."

As Ryan dashed over the rocks in the cove, he wondered whether he had done the right thing in telling his teacher all about Pirate. He especially feared that the children would find out about his friend's existence. The cove was out of bounds to small children, but some of the older ones played on the beaches nearby. Ryan didn't intend to share Pirate with anyone.

Within seconds of Ryan reaching the water's edge, Pirate shot through the waves like a rocket. His eye patch showed up clearly against his light grey face, which wore its usual comical smile. The Frisbee was between his jaws, but playing with it was not what he had in mind. Instead, he swam out further from the shore and barked at Ryan. The boy was confused. Pirate swam even further away from the shore, dropped the Frisbee, leaving it to float on the water, and barked louder and more persistently.

"What's up, Pirate?" Ryan shouted across the waves. More barks were the seal's reply. Acting on a sudden impulse, Ryan bent down and removed his shoes and socks then, rolling up his trousers, waded into the sea. Barks of approval exploded like loud laughter into the air. "Is *that* it? You want me to join you?"

Pirate was delighted, nodding his head and still barking. Ryan splashed back to the shore and rummaged in his school bag until he produced a pair of games shorts. As soon as he had changed into them, he rushed into the water and swam confidently to Pirate's side. At last the seal was quiet; he had achieved his goal. Ryan was in the sea with him: his domain.

Ryan marvelled as Pirate performed a series of manoeuvres: swimming at speed, leaping and rolling over and over, and at one point, diving for long enough to make Ryan wonder whether his friend had left the cove. Much to Ryan's delight, the seal suddenly popped up right next to him.

When Pirate headed for a group of rocks situated to one side of the cove, Ryan followed. Although the water was fairly shallow, Ryan was worried about the way the waves seemed to be driving him against the rocks. He was a competent swimmer for his age, and a safe swimmer, because he knew how easily the sea could change moods. It could endanger even the strongest. Pirate sensed that Ryan felt uneasy and led him round to the other side of the rocks. There, the water was calmer. Pirate dived, and within a few seconds, surfaced next to Ryan. The seal barked, encouraging his friend to follow him below. It wasn't very deep and even though Ryan lacked a face mask, it was just about clear enough for him to see the bottom with all its wonderful features. Everywhere, brilliant Jewel Anemones and Cup Coral studded the rocky ledges – an underwater garden. Ryan thought it was beautiful – as though he had stumbled upon sunken treasure.

He surfaced and dived three more times with Pirate, who seemed to enjoy acting as guide in his kingdom beneath the waves. Ryan could make out the seal's form underwater as Pirate glided with ease over the sea-bed, or sped past him so fast that he felt pulled along by the rush of water flowing in the seal's wake. It had always amused Ryan how clumsy and lumbering seals appeared to be on land; now he had seen one moving below the water, he realized they possessed all the grace of ballerinas. Ryan wondered what it would feel like to be a seal; to close off his nostrils and his ears so he could dive to great depths. There, big bright eyes and sensitive whiskers could detect fish – and catch them!

Pirate was eager to move on and reveal more secrets of his world to Ryan. He surfaced, barked, and headed off in another direction. Ryan had been close behind him and floated on the water for a while to rest. Pirate turned and, seeing his friend lying on his back, rushed to his side. "Just give me a few moments to get my breath back," Ryan puffed. "You were made to move at speed in the sea, but you wouldn't stand a chance against me on land!"

It was only a little way to the next destination in Pirate's undersea excursion. When

they dived, it was still shallow and clear enough for Ryan to see. They landed on the remains of an old fishing boat. So fascinated by all he saw, Ryan held his breath far too long and was forced to surface, gulping in lungfuls of air. He rested a while, then dived once again, with Pirate close by his side. Ryan watched in amazement as the seal took advantage of an early supper on offer. Craftily, he pursued little fishes in and out of the boat's wheelhouse. The poor creatures didn't stand a chance against the skilful fisherman.

Ryan's eyes had begun to sting from the salty water. He realized he needed the aid of a face mask to really explore the wreck. Quickly, before he surfaced, he let his hands explore the rotting beams of wood which crumbled easily beneath his touch. Everywhere, different forms of sea life had made the wreck their home: anemones, spider crabs, sponges of many varieties – even Ryan's favourite, Dead Man's fingers, a sort of coral that actually resembles the long, white fingers of a dead man.

Ryan surfaced and shivered. The air had chilled. Above, the sky had begun to change to the pinky blue of early evening. Pirate suddenly erupted through the water. Freshly nourished by his snack, he was ready to continue the tour. Regrettably, Ryan realized it was time for him to head for home and indicated his intention to Pirate, who joined him on the shore. Ryan wished he could stay with Pirate all of the time. On the shore, he attempted to dry himself with the aid of a grubby sock found at the bottom of his school bag. He thanked Pirate for showing him his world beneath the waves, as the seal lay in the gentle surf, sweeping over his rounded, shiny form. He stretched, inspected his flippers and yawned. Before moving off, Ryan gently patted Pirate's head. In return, the seal gave a friendly bark and watched Ryan stride to the top of the path, where he turned to wave.

The walk back to Lighthouse Cottage made Ryan's legs ache. Swimming and diving with Pirate required a great deal of exertion from tired and aching muscles. But Ryan was comfortably tired and glowed with a happiness he hadn't felt in a long time. He knew he was privileged to have a friend like Pirate – a very special friend.

Chapter 3

By the time Ryan had reached Lighthouse Cottage he felt fit to burst with excitement. He needed to tell someone about his afternoon with Pirate. It would have to be his father. Even if he appeared to be too busy to listen, or he was in one of his miserable moods, which seemed to be more frequent of late, he would still try to talk to him.

Hurling his soggy bag into the porch, Ryan crashed through the kitchen door, shouting, "Guess what, Dad!" Hardly had the words left his lips, than his face froze. Seated at the table was Matthew Thorpe, his head bowed over an old photograph album. Ryan saw that it was open on a page filled with pictures of his mother. He went over to his father, closed the album, and placed it in a drawer.

"Dad, this isn't doing you any good. *Mum's gone!* I know you miss her – don't you think *I* do too? But this is horrid and morbid. She wouldn't have wanted it. Why don't you pay *me* some attention for a change, instead of living in the past with a lot of old photographs?"

Matthew Thorpe made no attempt to answer Ryan, not even when his son, obviously upset, swept across the room to the stairs. He ran up to his bedroom, already regretting his words to his father. Inside his room, he threw himself on to his bed feeling very confused: sorry for his father, and yet very angry with him. Ryan couldn't understand why his dad had shut him out of his life since the death of his mother. He had been such a good father before her death; now, he had no interest in him. An awful thought occurred to Ryan: perhaps his father would have preferred him to have gone, and not his mother.

Ryan stood up and faced the window. He could see the waves rolling towards the island. That evening, they failed to calm him. Ryan's thoughts ran to Pirate. He wished he could dive with the seal and surface in another land, far away from the island. He wanted to flee Lighthouse Cottage for ever.

Downstairs, Matthew banged shut the front door and made his way to the only inn on the island. Ryan also sought freedom from the suffocating atmosphere of the cottage. He wandered down to the cove – Pirate's cove, as he had come to think of it. The light was fading and the rocks felt cold as he lowered himself on to one at the water's edge. On the horizon the sky was pink and brown. Bright little spots of light twinkled on the mainland across the water. Behind Ryan, midnight-blue sky crept slowly over the island. He wondered where his friend Pirate was at that moment: perhaps sleeping safe and warm as part of a seal colony. It was peaceful sitting there thinking about his friend, as the water gradually crept around his ankles. It didn't bother Ryan at all that his shoes and feet were soaking wet.

There was little light left when Ryan decided to return home. As he sat wringing sea water out of his trouser bottoms, he heard a familiar bark from the waves. Peering closely at the black water, the fading light just caught the top of Pirate's head.

"What's *this*?" Ryan exclaimed, surprised by the sudden appearance of his friend. "Don't you have a real home to go to either? Or are you just restless tonight?" The seal flopped clumsily over the sand and pebbles to rest at Ryan's feet, like a faithful dog. His huge eyes looked up at Ryan, who wrapped his arms around him, hugging him and breathing in the sharp saltiness of the seal's smooth skin.

A chilly breeze from the sea reminded Ryan that it was time to return home. He released the seal's slippery neck from his grasp.

"I wish I could join you and swim away to wherever it is that you go." He smiled at the seal, who blinked affectionately back at him, before returning to the water and sinking beneath the waves.

High up on the cliffs, despite the fading light, Miss Roberts had witnessed the tender scene between her pupil and the seal.

Chapter 4

Ryan began to spend far less time at home, choosing instead to wander the shores, climb the rocks or, best of all, be with Pirate. Every day, the seal presented himself in the cove for a game with the well-chewed Frisbee, and Ryan looked forward to those times more than anything else.

Pirate had learned to respond readily to his name and as soon as Ryan called, the seal would usually appear. He wondered whether Pirate spent the greater part of his life cruising the waters of the cove, in the hope of a game with the Frisbee. But at the end of the day, Ryan often observed that he swam off towards the tip of the island. Around it lay the more rugged side, where he imagined Pirate probably lived in a colony.

Ryan became curious about Pirate's life when he was away from him. In the books at school, he had read how seals needed to catch plentiful supplies of fish. For this reason, their bodies were made for speed and efficiency in the water and were capable of diving deep to catch their food. The females reared their young with great tenderness, keeping them close until they were strong and confident enough to brave the water, which the pups did very early in life. At times, other females would help rear and protect the seal pups, often rescuing them from the rolling waves that crashed against the rocks, capable of sweeping a little one away.

Keen to observe the seals around the island and hopeful of catching sight of Pirate amongst them, Ryan woke early one Saturday morning. He borrowed one of his father's dinghies with an outboard motor. Carefully he navigated the tip of the island, steering well clear of the dangerous rip tides around a group of rocks further out to sea. In the distance he saw some seals gathered on a large, flat slab of rock. As he moved closer, he was shocked to find they were motionless. Were they dead? Panicking, he revved up the engine. He was relieved when, lazily, they stirred themselves. A few rolled over on to their backs, exposing huge bellies covered in freckles; others attempted to bark before falling asleep again. Ryan left them to dream about their next meals.

Further up the rugged side of the island, he spied another group. Here, they appeared to be more active. Several young seals of Pirate's age and size were resting. A little way off, some mothers were fussing over their pups who wanted to be up and away, instead of being groomed. But the ones who really held Ryan's attention were two great, battle-scarred bull seals. Cautiously he moved nearer. They responded by manoeuvring their huge, blubbery hulks to the edge of the water for a better look at the intruder. Once they had established he was staying put, and of no immediate threat, they moved away to settle a score as to who ranked supreme leader of the colony. Both opened their mouths wide to display bright red interiors. With heads thrown back, they roared loud enough to make the little ones snuggle closer to their mothers' sides. One bull seal had more scars and wrinkles; trophies of past battles.

Ryan was gripped by the drama of the scene. He sensed something was about to happen. Was the less scarred of the two, the one who appeared to be the challenger, going to back down and move away? Warily, they eyed one another. Suddenly and without warning, the less scarred lunged at his opponent's neck, sinking his teeth into rubbery flesh. Like Sumo wrestlers, their hulks locked in combat. Both then sank teeth into flesh resembling elephant's hide, with great roars of pain ensuing. Tirelessly the warriors fought on, their battle cries echoing around the cliffs, until the less scarred challenger, sensing victory only moments away, raised his head proudly towards the rest of the colony. He had presumed too soon. The crafty old bull unexpectedly summoned energy and strength enough for a last mighty charge. With all the force he could muster, he hurled himself at the other, and with sheer brute strength pushed and shoved his opponent into the water – and into submission. Another battle won – but how many more until a challenger proved too strong and agile for the aging beast?

The spectacle had Ryan rooted to the spot, wondering what would happen next. The females and the younger seals seemed to show little, if any, interest. For the mothers especially, the sight of two vast males fighting for supremacy hardly rated a second look. They were more concerned with rearing champions of the future, licking and preening the fluffy little pups into shape. Soon the young ones would exchange the silky fur for tougher skin that would harden and dry with age.

Ryan prepared to move away, his eyes

sweeping over the scene, taking in a glorious picture of the seals he would never forget. All ages of the wonderful creatures were represented; from tiny pups to the wizened old bulls. Ryan noticed a small cluster of younger seals at the back of the group, not far off adulthood. His eyes were drawn to one in particular who was easily recognizable by a black mark over one eye. Pirate had seen Ryan but chose to lower his head, as though not wishing to be acknowledged by the boy. Ryan realized that Pirate, when in the confines of the colony, came under its elders – and its leader, who was still displaying his pride as a victor. No one moved until he was ready to rest.

Ryan felt strange to be so near to his friend Pirate, who had to remain detached. If Ryan attempted to move any nearer, he would probably need to contend with the ferocious old bull who continued wobbling his massive bulk in Ryan's direction, declaring his triumph and baring a mouth full of teeth, freshly stained with the blood of his opponent. Ryan glanced at Pirate and the seal blinked affectionately back at him – but that was all. One day Pirate would be a fully matured adult, in search of a mate; until then, he would return to the safety and protection of the colony.

During Ryan's journey around the island he sighted a few other groups of seals. Some were engaged in fishing, others lay on the rocks preening themselves like overweight old ladies, basking in the sun at a holiday resort.

He steered the dinghy towards the landing beach. Surprised, he saw Pirate, waiting for him a little way off the shore. Bobbing up and down in the waves, he issued an occasional friendly bark.

"So!" said Ryan. "You managed to slip away from that old brute. Promise me, Pirate, you'll never make him angry? He's got a mean temper and big teeth. I'd hate him to use them on you." Pirate dropped his head on one side and barked as though agreeing with Ryan.

Ryan felt hot and sticky, as if there was a storm on the way. He decided to cool off by joining Pirate in the water. Once he had beached the dinghy, he ran up to the boat-house and, after some rummaging, reappeared with a mask, snorkel and pair of fins. He sat at the edge of the water putting on the diving gear. Entering the water, he felt instantly cooled and refreshed. He splashed about, scooping great armfuls of water over Pirate, who circled round and round Ryan before diving. Looking through the mask at the water below, Ryan found the view so much clearer. The fins also helped him to keep up with Pirate most of the time and the snorkel allowed him to cruise along the surface of the water, while looking beneath him.

The seal appeared to be leading Ryan towards the tip of the island. Ryan was pre-pared to turn back; the currents there were far too strong for him. He stopped, and Pirate, realizing Ryan's hesitation, surfaced. The seal suddenly barked and took a turn towards a nearby cove. Stopping just short of it, he barked again, this time louder. Several rocks rose up from the water, barring Ryan's view of what lay behind. Pirate's barks were answered by a chorus of other seals from somewhere within the cove. Pirate urged Ryan to follow him into the enclosure. From behind their rocky fortress, several seals emerged, all about the same size and age as Pirate. When they saw Ryan, they lunged their heads at him, swaying from side to side, adopting a defensive attitude until they were reassured by Pirate that the stranger posed no threat. Once they had calmed down, Pirate dived beneath the water. In a few seconds he had surfaced with a fish in his mouth. Soon the others joined him to fish in the secluded waters of the cove.

At first Ryan floated on the surface of the water, looking through the mask at the action below. Just in that position, he was able to see a great deal. Fish were fleeing in all directions with the seals in hot pursuit. Ryan thought it better than any film he had seen of underwater creatures. The mask made everything so clear.

Unable to resist the temptation to be part of the frenzied chase below, he dived to join them and become part of the action. The seals were all around him, no longer bothered in the least by his presence. Several times he spotted Pirate, sleek and fast in his movements. Ryan marvelled at the speed and accuracy of the creatures. He felt water rushing in the wake of them as they sped past. One seal, close on the tail of its unfortunate prey, came dashing towards Ryan like a gigantic bullet; Ryan was petrified it wouldn't stop, confused as to which way he should go to avoid being hit. At the very last moment, the seal swerved to one side and claimed the fish, but not before brushing against Ryan and knocking off his mask. Hurriedly he surfaced and took some breaths before replacing it.

Ryan went below the surface once again. He realized that the action was beginning to slow down and soon the seals would finish fishing. Just once more he wanted to experience the sheer pleasure of being surrounded

by the wonderful animals. He noticed how their silvery skins reflected shafts of light penetrating the water, and marvelled at the speed with which they seemed to suddenly materialize from the deep, green water beyond his vision. Ryan attempted to copy their movements. With arms clamped at his sides and his legs close together, he used the rubber fins on his feet to propel himself through the water. He felt clumsy in the seals' environment, as he tried to chase after fish. They escaped him with ease, only to be caught by the expert fishermen around them.

Ryan tired before the seals had finished dining. Slowly he began to fin his way back to the shore. As he flopped down at the water's edge and began removing his fins, mask and snorkel, he was joined by Pirate.

"*That* must be one of the greatest moments in my life, Pirate. Thank you for taking me fishing." He bent and squeezed the seal's neck in a friendly hug. "I'll see you tomorrow."

Ryan gathered his gear and started off across the rocks towards the cottage. Pirate halted for a few seconds, before rejoining the other seals, who had surfaced and were heading for the rocks where they would first clean their whiskers, then sleep.

Chapter 5

Ryan opened the back door to the cottage, prepared this time, if necessary, to force his father to listen to every detail of his exciting day. But there was no sign of Matthew. Instead, Ryan came upon a hastily-written note in his father's spidery hand-writing, propped up against the teapot. It explained that a bad storm was forecast, and expected to hit the island late that evening. The note went on to say his father had gone to make an emergency repair in the glass surrounding the old light. Ryan's thoughts immediately ran to Pirate. He hoped he would shelter somewhere safe. He had seen the havoc caused by storms before when they hit the island.

Since the old lighthouse had become automatic there had been very little Matthew had to do apart from ensuring that its structure was preserved. During his last inspection of the tower, Matthew had noticed a slight crack in one of the glass panes. To do the job properly would require replacing the glass, but the crack was very slight, and more urgent jobs had required attendance. Until the storm warning, he had put the repair further down his list of priorities. The threat of blinding rain and fierce gales made him unable to rest until a temporary repair had been made. The efficiency of the light and foghorns was vital to shipping. The great tankers and the small private crafts all benefited from the old lighthouses, no matter how sophisticated the tracking equipment they carried on board.

Before he left to make the repair, Matthew telephoned the farmers on the island and contacted the fishermen. The farmers needed to ensure their livestock were safely sheltered from gales which could be capable of sweeping cattle over the cliffs into the sea. Taking a bag of tools and some strong bonding adhesive, Matthew had climbed the winding staircase to the top of the lighthouse. It was a very tall tower which adjoined the cottage. Both were situated close to the cliffs which fell away to a rocky shoreline and the sea.

At the top of the staircase a door opened on to a narrow balcony running precariously around the great light. The door slammed shut behind Matthew, demonstrating the force the wind had already reached. The sky had begun to darken with grey clouds like smoke. Soon the great light would automatically turn itself on. Matthew knew he had to work fast, or the blindingly bright flashes from it would make his task very difficult. He inspected the crack; it was very small but still he felt he couldn't ignore it. Skilfully he squeezed adhesive through the nozzle into the crack and smoothed the surface with a little knife. The special adhesive would take ten minutes to bond.

Matthew felt rain on his face. At first it fell hesitantly, then in torrents, as the sky changed to a muddy brown. Matthew pulled up the collar of his coat and looked up at the clouds. Seagulls wheeled above him, sounding their alarm calls; perhaps warning their families to take to the cliffs. In the distance he heard the rumble of thunder announce its part in the approaching storm. Matthew made a rapid inspection of the rest of the glass panes for any other cracks that may have appeared, then returned to the repair. Satisfied that it had set solid, he quickly replaced his tools in the bag and was about to go downstairs, when, to his surprise, the door leading on to the balcony burst open to reveal Ryan standing breathless.

"Dad – the mainland coastguard has radioed over news of an oil spill out at sea. The tanker crew are safe, but the spill is estimated to be on course for the island. Unless the winds divert it, the oil will hit the top end of the island and spread down the other side where many of the seals live." Ryan had run up the giddily winding stairs, every breath stinging his chest.

"Oh, no!" exclaimed Matthew miserably. "That's all we need: storms, gales, fog, and now an oil spill! I must get to the radio in case further news of the oil comes over. Although there's little we can do if it does hit us." Grabbing his toolbag he headed for the stairs, calling out, "Ryan, don't hang about up here."

Ryan crouched down for a few moments to catch his breath after the long ascent. He noticed his father had left the big tube of adhesive on the balcony. The wind was gathering force, so Ryan grasped the balcony rail for support and held on tight as he guided his hand, stretching it as far as possible, towards the tube. He could feel the force of the wind desperately trying to drag him off and had almost reached it, when a mighty gust tore it from his grasp. Ryan watched it fall over the edge but didn't hear it drop way down on to the rocks below. He shivered, realizing just how near to the edge of the balcony he had moved, and cautiously shifted his way back to the doorway to return downstairs.

The thought of oil moving near the shores where Pirate lived had Ryan's mind working overtime for the seal's safety. Ryan caught up with his father in the cottage, just in time to hear a radio announcement: oil would be with them before midnight. Tentatively, Ryan asked his father if anything could be done to prepare the animals around the shores for a possible disaster. His father's reply sounded stern but he spoke from experience, and he spoke the truth.

"The birds and the seals will take care of themselves as best they can. Some may survive, others – if the oil is particularly heavy – won't make it. It's disastrous – but these things continue to happen. There's no way we can round up all the creatures and save them."

"But Dad," pleaded Ryan. "There's a *special* seal out there – he's my friend, Pirate. We've got to save him. Please help me look for him."

Matthew Thorpe looked at the distraught expression on his son's face. "Calm down, Ryan. I've got to contact the fishermen again to warn them about the oil. We don't want them stuck out at sea in a storm, with oil around. They depend on me to keep them informed."

"And *I* depend upon *Pirate*! He listens to me when *you're* too busy, or your mind is somewhere else."

Ryan had thrust his face up close to his father as he spoke the last sentence. For one fleeting moment, concern for his son's predicament showed on Matthew's face and he spoke quietly to Ryan.

"If, as you say, he's an especially clever seal, I'm sure he will find shelter until any danger is over." Matthew had seen the destruction oil pollution could bring to a coastline. The wildlife rarely escaped injury but some survived.

He contacted the fishermen to let them know of the spill. Most had heard from the coastguards and were returning immediately to the island, before the storm made their journey perilous. Then he telephoned his nearest neighbours, who were farmers, warning them of the strength the wind was expected to reach. Their farm was close to the cliffs and all livestock needed to be secure and sheltered for an even rougher night than first expected.

Ryan felt useless, sitting around the cottage while the wind howled and thunder crashed outside. High above him the foghorns blasted out their warning. What could he do to warn Pirate? He trudged up to his bedroom and stood looking out of the window at the sea below, angrily hurling itself at the little island. As the waves grew in size, Ryan feared more for Pirate. He reached up to close the curtains, to shut out the storm. As he did so, a brilliant flash of lightning lit up the water below. For an instant Ryan thought he saw several seals battling through the waves. A crash of thunder followed.

Ryan almost flew downstairs, passing his father in his urgency to get into waterproofs and go out into the gale.

Matthew halted his conversation on the telephone and spun round to watch his son. "Where on *earth* do you think you're off to?" he called.

"There are *seals* in the water; I've just seen them. One could be *Pirate*." Before his father had a chance to grab him, Ryan was off out of the back door. Matthew finished his conversation with the farmer by telling him he was going to fetch Ryan, as the foolish boy had run out into the storm to help some seals.

Outside, the wind almost blew Ryan off his feet. Unsure as to how exactly he could help the creatures, he nevertheless fought his way through the fierce gale and rain, aiming for the spot beneath his window where he had seen the seals. He kept close to the lighthouse, aware of just how near he was to the edge of the cliffs. His small pocket torch did little to help him see through the patches of fog drifting in from the sea. Behind him he could hear the distant voice of his father calling his name. Somewhere below, he heard another voice – the very familiar bark of a seal.

Ryan took a deep breath and called, "*Pirate!*" A hoarse bark came back, and with it, on the wind, drifted the sickly smell of oil. As forecast, the slick had arrived. From the top end of the island, it had drifted down, spreading its intrusive arms into all the coves and inlets where the seals and birds lived. Lightning flashed again, illuminating the scene below. The seals were making slow progress in thick, black, slimy water. Ryan couldn't distinguish Pirate from the others, but guessed he was the one out in front, leading them to his cove, in the hope of shelter and safety on the big rocks there.

Ryan heard his father call again. He was gaining on him. Showing little fear for his life, Ryan lay down and pulled himself to the edge of the cliff face. Lowering himself over, he used his feet to feel for footholds, while his hands gripped tufts of grass on top of the cliff. He was terrified. The cliffs were the height of two tall houses and he was scared to look down to see where best to place his feet.

As he dug his nails into the cliff face, chunks of it crumbled, tumbling to the rocks below. Slowly and cautiously, Ryan made his way down, despite the high wind desperately trying to tear him off.

Directly above him, Matthew repeatedly called Ryan's name and shone the powerful beam from his torch over the rocks and cliff below. As Ryan groped for another handhold, the torch beam picked him out. Matthew saw him and anxiously bellowed, "*Stay there, son.* I'm coming to get you!"

Ryan, desperate to reach the bottom, ignored his father's call and hurriedly placed his toes in a tiny crevice for support. He looked up, to see whether Matthew had started to climb down. He was already over the edge and had turned to shine the beam on Ryan, to ensure he was moving towards him.

As Ryan looked up for a second, he was dazzled by the brilliant beam. He felt giddy and the sound of Pirate's bark mingled with his father's voice in his ears. He tried to shut out the sounds and the bright light while he

reached out for another handhold, but missed.

Ryan fell, calling Pirate's name. When he landed, his body lay still and silent...

Chapter 6

On a rock below the cliffs where the waves were just out of reach, Ryan lay crumpled and terrified. Dreadful pain throbbed in his head and one of his shoulders.

In the torch beam, Matthew had seen his son fall. Without hesitation, he moved faster, groping wildly for handholds and footholds on his hazardous climb down. Desperate to reach Ryan, he silently prayed as he descended.

Pirate had heard Ryan shriek his name high above the sound of the waves and wind, and had heard the note of terror in the boy's voice as he fell. Still struggling in a mess of turbulent, oily water, the seal changed direction, leaving the others and heading to where he had heard the cry.

Like a bundle of old clothes, Ryan lay at the mercy of the waves which were moving nearer to him by the moment, keen to claim him. One huge wave rolled towards him and succeeded in partly dragging him off the rock he clung to with one frozen hand. Half of Ryan lay on the rock while the other flopped about like a broken doll in the angry sea. Ryan tried to pull himself back on to the rock before the next group of waves carried him off. But he was too weak to lift himself. He did all he was able to help himself, digging his fingers deep into a crevice and steeling himself to take the impact of the massive wave rushing open-mouthed towards him.

Ryan could feel the oily, salty breath of the wave in his nostrils. He breathed in deeply just before it struck, sensing from the incredible power of the water that it was probably his last breath. The polluted water filled his ears, eyes and mouth, and he could feel each finger as it was wrenched from the rock. Then, just as he felt himself slipping into the clutches of the sea, he suddenly experienced a sensation at his back, lifting him, bearing him upwards. As the wave receded he could still feel the forcc of something moving him back to the rock and supporting him. He gulped down air and

lunged with both arms at the slab of rock. His injured shoulder caused him to scream out with pain, but his fingers frantically sought out holes and crevices again, wedging themselves just before the next wave struck.

Ryan had no time to consider what it was that eagerly attempted to push him out of the water, while the sea seemed so intent upon drawing him in and below. He could sense the strength of the next enormous wave as it rushed towards him, at the same time as a mighty nudge at his back pushed him up and on to the rock. He clung to his life by his fingertips, the water gurgling over, around and beneath him. When the wave receded, Ryan raised his head enough to gulp in more air. Above the sound of rushing water he heard a familiar cry. It was Pirate's bark. Ryan turned his head in the direction of the sound, and, to his horror, saw the seal borne away on the wave, amongst debris of plastic bottles, driftwood and old cans. The sea seemed to have dredged up unwanted rubbish in order to hurl it back at the land.

Ryan realized that it had been Pirate at his back, lifting and supporting him until he had been able to get a hold on the rock. He also knew Pirate must have left his companions, to risk his life to save him.

Ryan used the opportunity Pirate had given him – another chance to live. Despite the terrible pain in his head and shoulder, he managed to roll over and over towards the cliffs, until he fell into a little gully. The waves could still reach him, but by gulping air before they struck, he was able to keep from being dragged out to sea again.

Soon exhaustion, cold, pain and the effort of fighting for air were too much for him. Ryan's vision blurred, and all sound faded as he slipped from consciousness.

Chapter 7

Matthew fought against the wind which blew stinging, salty spray into his face until his feet touched the rocks at the bottom of the cliffs. The strong beam from his torch swept over the rocks. Soon, more light was provided by Matthew's neighbours, the farmer and his son who, sensing all wasn't well when Matthew fled to fetch Ryan back, searched around the outside of the lighthouse and shone their torches on the cliffs below, calling to Matthew.

Now three beams of light played across the fierce shoreline. But it was by chance that Ryan was found, when his father stumbled and fell into the gully where his son lay. Kneeling down, with waves crashing about them, Matthew immediately checked to see that Ryan was breathing. Relieved to find that the freezing, battered bundle was still alive, he shouted to the men on the clifftop to fetch some board or a ladder, and strong rope; something to provide a makeshift stretcher to lift Ryan.

While Matthew waited for the men to return, he protected his son from the waves, using his own body as a barrier. He looked at the badly bruised face of his child and felt a sharp pang of guilt. He had become a stranger to the boy who chose to wander the island's coves and beaches, avoiding life at home. Matthew felt dreadful when he realized that it had taken the terrible shock of the accident for him to see how much he loved Ryan. All he wanted was a chance to make up for neglecting him for so long. He bent and kissed Ryan's oil-stained forehead.

What seemed like ages to Matthew was in fact only ten minutes, before the farmer and his son returned to lower a ladder attached to strong ropes. They had also brought a large lantern which cast a brilliant light over the scene below. The waves still lashed the rocks and both Matthew and Ryan were completely soaked. Hurriedly, Matthew manoeuvred the limp form of his son on to the ladder and bound him to it tightly with the rope. A tug on the rope and a shout from Matthew, alerted the men to start the long haul up the cliff face. Matthew climbed close to Ryan, guiding the ladder when the wind swung it too far out from the cliff, and freeing it when it occasionally caught against an outcrop of rock.

Matthew's fingers and knees were raw from the scramble down, and now they were deeply cut in places from the ascent, but the cold helped numb the pain. Just over halfway up, Ryan recovered from the deep faint that had removed him from the dreadful experience of the last hour or so. He could feel himself being raised upwards to the dark, clouded night sky, without even a star to comfort him.

He was terrified, unable to fathom what was happening. He screamed, "*Dad!*" and in reply his father hauled himself up next to him.

"Ryan, don't be afraid, you're safe. We're moving up the cliffs and we're nearly at the top." The wind carried the last of his words away but Ryan understood and closed his eyes. A few more bumps near the top, and, with Matthew adding support to the ladder from below, Ryan was lifted efficiently over the clifftop on to the grass. A blanket was laid over him and a cushion eased beneath his head. One of the men had already alerted the helicopter rescue service, who said they would be with them as soon as the fog had lifted a little more for them to take off.

True to their words, the rescue service soon announced itself with a thudding of helicopter blades in the sky. Matthew and the men moved Ryan out to a flat grassy space at the side of the cottage, as there was nowhere the helicopter could land for some distance and they knew it would be quicker to winch

him up. Matthew knelt by his son's side and asked him where he felt pain. Ryan was shivering so much he could hardly answer. A man was winched down and Matthew quickly told him where Ryan's injuries appeared to be. Together they transferred Ryan to a stretcher attached to the winch. Slowly, Ryan and the rescue man rose upwards and into the helicopter. Matthew was then hauled up to join them.

The helicopter flew over the angry sea below, which from above appeared to be boiling with rage. A medic on board checked Ryan's blood pressure, looked at his injuries, and shone a torch as slim as a pencil into each eye, jotting down any observations. Matthew asked if he could hold his son's hand, and Ryan didn't wait for the man to answer, as he poked shaky, bruised fingers from beneath the blanket. Matthew received them into the palms of his hands and gently warmed them.

With the brief examination over, Matthew enquired softly, "He will be all right, won't he?"

"Your son will be in the best possible hands the minute we get him to casualty," the man replied. "What on earth was he doing near the cliffs on a night like this?"

"He ran out into the storm to save a seal he had befriended," Matthew answered sadly. "I ran after him, but he had started to climb down the cliff face. My torch light picked him out but must have dazzled him. That's when he fell. I tried to keep the beam on him as I climbed down, but for some time he was completely lost to me. I'll swear he was dragged into the water. That's why he has patches of vile oil on him from the slick. To be honest, I just don't know how he survived."

"Your son must have been very attached to that seal. Shame, with all that oil around, there's going to be less of them about the island after tonight," said the medic, shaking his head.

On reaching hospital, Ryan was rushed straight to casualty. Lights flashed, buzzers buzzed and efficient nurses dashed to receive the young emergency patient. Matthew, his face haggard and grey, stayed with Ryan, holding his hand until one of the doctors explained that Ryan would be undergoing some tests. It would probably be better if a nurse cleaned up Matthew's wounds and got him something warm to drink, while he waited until they had a clearer picture of Ryan's injuries.

Matthew was led into a cubicle where the nurse carefully removed little slithers of chalk and grit from beneath the skin of both his palms and knees. He was shown to a small room equipped with a bed, and given a hot drink. At last he lay down to rest his bruised limbs and aching muscles, stiff with fatigue. But the only pain that troubled him came from the uncertainty of Ryan's condition. Massive waves of guilt washed over him when he considered how little he knew of his son's daily existence. "Pirate is my *only* friend!" Ryan's words came back to disturb Matthew as his heavy eyelids closed and visions of his son lying as though lifeless returned to haunt him.

Matthew Thorpe hated himself. He had been so blinded by grief that he'd excluded his own son from his life. The dreadful accident had thrust him back into living and caring again, instead of just existing. Ryan had been there, reaching out for his father to share his life, but the boy had met with nothing but disinterest. He hoped it wouldn't be too late to show Ryan how much he cared for him; that he had woken up as though from a long sleep to see his son for the first time in a long while.

Chapter 8

Somewhere above him, a voice seemed to be repeating, "Mr Thorpe, Mr *Thorpe*." Matthew had finally slept, and as he fought to open his eyes, the last remnants of a dream drifted away. He had been battling against an angry, oily sea to save Ryan, who was always just out of reach, no matter how hard he tried to stretch out to touch him.

Matthew sat bolt upright and looked at the nursing sister. "*Ryan!*" he exclaimed. "Is he all right?"

The sister put a hand on his shoulder. "He will be, Mr Thorpe. Would you like to see him?"

As they walked along the corridors, the sister explained that Ryan had a fractured skull and a lot of severe bruising and abrasions, especially around one shoulder. The doctor would give him more details later, but he would heal, given rest and time. She warned Matthew not to be too alarmed by the bruising and swelling on his son's face. It would subside as the weeks went by. It had been a miracle he had survived the accident so well. She told him that Ryan, although frozen from long exposure to the storm, hadn't as much as a runny nose.

Despite the sister's warning, Matthew wasn't quite prepared for the sight of Ryan's injuries. His face and eyes were puffed up, and the rest of his body was heavily bruised. Ryan tried to move his head to gain a better view of his father as he entered the room. "Sorry, Dad," was all he could manage to whisper. Matthew moved to Ryan's bedside and gently took his hand in his own.

"Ryan, *I'm* the one who should be apologizing. This dreadful ordeal has shaken me to my senses. I've realized you mean so much to me – and I could have lost you! Just give me a chance to make up for the misery I've caused."

He squeezed Ryan's hand affectionately. Ryan gave his father the best he could manage by way of a smile; his face and head throbbed with pain. One word fell from his lips – "Pirate?"

Matthew hadn't the heart to tell him that there was probably little chance the seal had survived, unless he had hidden himself somewhere safe from the stormy, oily sea.

"Dad, promise me you'll look for him – *he*

saved me! When I was in the sea, *he* stopped me from drowning by keeping me upright, pushing me against the rocks until I could pull myself on to them with his help."

Matthew realized he had been right in assuming his son had actually been in the sea. Incredible as it sounded, he believed his son and vowed that as soon as he returned to the island, he would move heaven and earth to find Pirate.

Matthew waited until Ryan's heavy eyelids closed and he drifted off to sleep, assured of his dad's intention to search for Pirate. As Matthew bent over to kiss him, he noticed a little tear in the corner of Ryan's eye. He knew it was for the seal.

Chapter 9

Two days later, after spending hours with Ryan, talking to him, reading to him, or just listening with interest as he related adventures he'd shared with Pirate, Matthew flew back to the island. Ryan needed fresh clothing and Matthew had to speak to the relief warden allocated his job until Ryan was able to return home.

As the helicopter landed, Matthew saw immediately signs of damage everywhere. The storm had hit the island just as surely as a marksman scoring a bull's-eye. Inland, fences, crops and even the island's electricity generator hadn't escaped harm. On the shores, damage caused by the oil slick was plain for all to see. Viewed from above, the island would appear to have a thick, black line around it. The islanders who lived closest to the shores found it difficult to avoid seeing defenceless wildlife victims, strewn along the rocks and beaches, claimed by the engulfing oil.

Dead or stranded sea birds littered the shores and the water close to them. Some of the larger sea birds stuck in the thick, treacle-like mess had died struggling to rise from it, and looked like shiny, black statues. Smaller birds had succumbed quickly. Hundreds of dead fish drifted back and forth on the tide, their dead eyes staring up at the sky. In its mission to destroy, it seemed as though the oil hadn't missed one variety of the creatures living on or around the shores. Predators and their prey rocked silently side by side on the sluggish tide, united in death by the same enemy.

Teams from animal rescue centres had been flown over from the mainland or arrived by boat. Equipped with cleansing agents, first aid materials and all that was necessary for performing minor surgery, they soon set about cleaning the hopeful cases, or painlessly destroying those unfortunates who were beyond help. As they travelled around the coastline, behind a group of experts called in to disperse the oil, the rescue volunteers noticed many seals affected and endangered by the spill. Some had taken the polluted water into their lungs, while others had been stranded with their young on the rocks. A few gasped their last breaths alone, too late for the rescuers. Mothers with pups sensed it would be wrong to subject their young to the water, so they had stayed marooned and hungry on the rocks, until the rescuers took them off to temporary seal pools, erected on the island's landing beach. Once settled, the seals found food and sanctuary until the sea water was declared safe enough for them to return to their colonies.

Once the long task of cleaning a seal had been successfully accomplished in the small pool, it was then released into a larger one where it could feed and swim. Fresh fish were delivered daily, and it didn't take the seals long to realize just who was feeding them. Whenever one of the rescue workers passed by, a chorus of barking seals echoed around the beach. Sometimes the anticipated fish would appear; if not, the seals would stare after the passer-by, and then at one another, with deeply offended looks on their whiskered faces.

A boat had taken a few young seals and several orphaned pups to a mainland seal sanctuary. There, they were able to receive the special nurturing the very young ones needed.

The islanders rallied to help Matthew in every way possible. Miss Roberts cleaned the cottage and kept the larder well stocked, so that Matthew could feed himself between crossings to and from the hospital.

Whenever Ryan saw his father, he asked for any news or sightings of Pirate. Matthew wished more than anything he could bring good news of the seal. He had asked the rescue workers dealing with the seals whether they had come across one with the distinctive eye patch that Pirate displayed, but no one had seen a seal of that description.

With every enquiry, Matthew's hopes of finding Pirate faded, although he refused to give in until he had explored every possibility. If the seal was reported dead, then at least there would be a conclusion to the sad matter. It was not knowing the seal's fate that frustrated Matthew, and distressed Ryan so much.

Taking a dinghy one morning, Matthew set off around the island in search of the creature so precious to his son. Passing the cliffs where Ryan had fallen made him shiver. It seemed so peaceful; hard to imagine the night the sea had lashed the island for almost twelve hours, bringing with it a deadly cargo of oil. Matthew increased his speed and had soon travelled about halfway up one side of the island. He became aware of the dinghy beginning to labour, realizing too late that he had run into a patch of oil lingering near a cove. The water moved sluggishly, and dozens of dead sea birds lay on the surface, or scattered about the rocks, like blackened, charred wood.

Matthew steered the dinghy towards the small cove, aware that it was the sort of place where seals might shelter. As he moved closer, adjusting his eyes to the shade, he gradually focused upon two dead seal pups, drifting with the movement of the tide. Their tiny bodies were covered in oil. The angry sea had probably washed them off the rocks on the night of the storm. Matthew was deeply saddened. As a warden, he had seen young animals lying dead on the island many times, but knowing his son's attachment and admiration for these creatures made the sight all the more poignant. He moved off along the coast, occasionally seeing a few seals tentatively edging their way towards the water, at the sound of the approaching engine. They appeared to Matthew to be in good condition, unaffected by the oil. Perhaps these had sheltered safely throughout the disaster. His hopes for Pirate were raised. Rescue workers visited them twice a day to feed fresh fish, enabling them to thrive. These were the lucky ones. Matthew studied their features carefully but not one with a black eye patch was to be seen.

Having completed a full circuit of the island and seeing only one more group of seals, Matthew headed for the landing beach to moor his dinghy. He arrived at the cottage to find Miss Roberts ironing fresh pyjamas for Ryan. Matthew would take them on his next visit to see his son. He wished he could take the news that Ryan so longed to hear.

Early next morning Matthew travelled over to the mainland, on the island supply ship. He took with him a small portable television, lent by one of the islanders, and lots of chocolates and specially-made get well cards from the children. As his father held up each item for Ryan to see, his son smiled. Matthew anticipated and dreaded the moment when Ryan would ask the inevitable question. It came. Had there been any sightings of a seal even remotely like Pirate? Matthew felt his heart sink, and found it hard to look at the eager expression on Ryan's face.

"I've searched high and low for your seal, Ryan. I've asked rescue workers, people at the seal sanctuary, even coastguards; so far, no one has seen Pirate. I'm sorry – I'll keep looking if you want me to, but it really looks as though he would have shown up by now."

"No. *No!* You think he's gone. You think he's *dead*, don't you? But it's not true. He's alive! I know it. I feel it!"

Ryan was fired with enthusiasm to recover and return to the island so he could search for Pirate. Throughout the following weeks, Ryan's injuries showed a great improvement and he became impatient to leave hospital. He still needed plenty of bed rest but as he gained in strength, the doctors were satisfied with him. Ryan was permitted to walk about the children's wards. He spoke to other children but had no interest in striking up friendships – he wanted to be out!

Almost a month to the day of the accident, Ryan was discharged. His father was so pleased. At last a trip to hospital to fetch Ryan home. The fracture was still healing and anything strenuous had to be avoided. No running, swimming, climbing; in fact, everything that Ryan usually enjoyed was forbidden.

When Ryan arrived home, it was to a different atmosphere from the one he had learned to avoid. The cottage welcomed him and seemed light and airy. Matthew had worked hard to make it that way. Up in his bedroom, he gazed out of the window. The late afternoon sun made patches of the sea look like molten gold. It looked so beautiful that Ryan found it hard to imagine how he had stared out at the sea below on the night of the storm, when it raged against the island. He stood and considered for a few moments how strange that the events of that dreadful night had given him back his father, but taken away the best friend he had ever known. Ryan tried to blot out the voice of doubt in his mind and be positive – keep on believing that Pirate would return. A whole month had gone by and lots of seals had returned to the water, but Pirate wasn't one of them.

Miss Roberts arrived at the cottage one morning to find Matthew excited. In his hand he held a letter; it had arrived that morning. Ryan had secured a place at the school of his choice on the mainland. When Matthew told Ryan he was pleased, but not ecstatic. Other things had come along to replace his longing for life on the mainland.

In the evening Ryan wanted to wander down to the cove where he had first met Pirate. Matthew agreed to him going but insisted on accompanying him. He reminded Ryan how wet and slippery the path could be; Ryan couldn't risk another fall. They walked in silence until they reached the cove.

"I really don't think you should go any further, the rocks are wet," Matthew advised.

"But *Dad*, please just help me to the edge of the water. I want to stand there for a few minutes and remember some of the times I spent with Pirate."

His father found it impossible to refuse him. "Hold on to me really tightly then. We'll take it very slowly."

With slow but careful progress they eventually made it to the water's edge, where Ryan stood on a familiar old rock. He stared out to where the horizon merged sea and sky. Happy memories flooded back. Ryan felt strange, almost as though he could sense the presence of the seal – or was it his ghost?

Then, from deep within him came a cry he had suppressed for weeks. "PIRATE! PIRATE! Where *are* you?" he shouted at the empty waves.

Matthew wrapped his arms around his son and hugged him, holding him tight while the boy sobbed loudly.

"It's not fair. It's just not fair." Ryan's words were muffled by his father's coat as he buried his face into it.

Together the pair moved towards the path. The excursion had tired and upset Ryan.

Having crossed the wet rocks, they started the long climb uphill. Matthew stopped and said to his son, "Did you hear that? I'll swear it was a seal barking. There's plenty of them back in the water now; perhaps you can find another friend among them."

The second the words had left his mouth, Matthew regretted them. He was at a loss as to how to comfort his son. They walked on together in silence, with the occasional bark of a seal coming from the cove. The barks continued. Deeper than Pirate's bark, they sounded more like the bark of an older seal. Even more barks followed and Ryan was tempted to turn and look; but felt unable to face the prospect of seeing a seal other than Pirate in the cove.

Chapter 10

Throughout the following weeks, Ryan and his father made return trips to hospital where the doctors were pleased with Ryan's progress. He had gained in strength enough to persuade his father he was capable of getting around by himself. He resumed his evening trips to the cove alone.

On one such evening he sat in his usual spot on the shore, recalling happy times spent with Pirate. Ryan had been trying desperately to accustom himself to life without the seal, but try as he might, a ray of hope still glimmered, hoping against all odds that the seal would return. Just news that he still lived would have satisfied Ryan for a while. Often, visions of the nightmarish storm returned to wake him in the night. It was his last sight of Pirate, caught up and borne away on the great, oily wave, that was so unbearable.

Ryan was determined to set his mind on other things – to concentrate on the future. He watched the last rays of the sun fade as he had done so many times with Pirate, then selected a flat pebble, stood up, and skimmed it across the surface of the water. "One, two, three … and a bit," he counted as the pebble bounced across the gentle waves. Turning away from the sea, Ryan made his way back across the rocks and began the well-worn route to the top of the path. About halfway, he paused for breath. Apart from the occasional squawk from a passing seagull, the island was peaceful – almost silent.

As Ryan started off again, a sudden noise intruded upon the peace. Instantly recognizing it to be another seal bark, he carried on walking. It came again. It too, like the one he had heard with his father, sounded deeper than Pirate's bark. Ryan carried on. He would have to get used to seals around and just accept that this was one of them, but not Pirate – his bark was higher, younger.

Ryan quickened his step, as the barking got louder. If he turned around now, he would spend the rest of his life looking over his shoulder every time a seal opened its mouth. But the barking was persistent. Ryan's head began to ache. He clamped his hands to his ears to drive out the sound, but it refused to go away.

Unable to resist any longer, and to prove that the deep bark wasn't Pirate's, despite its strange familiarity, Ryan turned to face the sea and direction of the noise. At first, all he saw was a flash of grey seal skin disappearing with a splash. It was followed by another splash, then another, as the creature moved too quickly for Ryan to discern any features. He began to walk back down the path, curious about the seal's display of activity in the water. A shiny head popped up from the little waves and sank back down just as quickly. Ryan felt strangely drawn to the sea. He slithered across the rocks on the shore until he stopped just short of the water.

All was silent again, but it was an odd silence that lingered in the cove, like the hush after lightning, before thunder. Even the gulls had stopped their screeching and taken to the cliffs, waiting, watching, sensing something was about to happen. Ryan's eyes were fixed on a place in the water where movement stirred below the surface. He stared as though hypnotized, hardly daring to breathe.

It happened in an instant. In a few seconds, peace was shattered and the silence broken, as the waters opened up at the exact spot Ryan watched so intently. A magnificent head burst through the waves, its mouth wide open, filling the air with a resounding bark that echoed around the cove. The noise forced the gulls to take off, shrieking a fanfare of welcome to a familiar character. PIRATE WAS BACK!

Ryan dashed fully clothed into the sea. Giving little thought to his promise to stay out of the water, he waded in up to his chest, then plunged and swam until he came face to face with his old friend. They stared at one another. Ryan was motionless, afraid to break the spell. He could hardly speak.

"Pirate," he whispered, "is it you? Is it really you, or am I dreaming?"

Pirate had grown big. His thick skin shone like pale steel in the evening light, making his black eye patch more obvious than ever. He had exchanged the appearance of an adolescent seal for a fully grown male, with a noticeably deeper bark. In no way did he resemble the old bull seals Ryan had seen, but Pirate had undoubtedly matured in his appearance. Ryan couldn't believe his eyes. Through tears of happiness he said, "I knew you'd come back – I never really gave up hope. You're the reason why I'm here and alive. You saved me, Pirate, and I'll never forget it."

A little way out to sea, the old Frisbee bobbed on the water. Pirate swam to it and hurled it to the shore. Ryan splashed back to retrieve it. As he bent to pick it up he noticed with sadness that it was stained with oil. Whatever ordeal Pirate must have undergone after Ryan had last seen him, he had somehow kept the old Frisbee with him.

Standing on the shore, dripping wet, Ryan tossed the Frisbee as far out to sea as possible. Pirate, as swift and agile as ever, dashed towards it. But it wasn't Pirate who rose to secure it between his jaws. Instead, another seal, a pretty female, leapt from the waves to snatch it out of the air. She gently played with it in the water for a while, nosing it along the surface, then rolling on to her back, and patting it along with a flipper. When she finally decided to toss it with her mouth, it was to Pirate that she sent the Frisbee whistling across the waves, so forcefully that he was forced to duck below the water for fear of it hitting him. He swam after it and sent it back to her. Ryan felt confused. He hadn't reckoned on competition for Pirate's affection. He had only ever wanted Pirate back; he wasn't too sure how he felt about sharing him. After a few moments' consideration, Ryan realized that having Pirate back again, safe and alive, was all that really mattered. The old Frisbee landed at his feet with a splash, inviting Ryan to become part of a fast game between the three of them.

Half an hour later, Ryan began to feel dizzy. It had been the first real exercise he had enjoyed but realized he would be foolish to overdo it. Reluctantly he called goodbye to Pirate and his lady friend, promising to return the next morning. Pirate barked his farewell as Ryan crossed the rocks. Still struggling to come to terms with all that had happened within the past hour, he stopped at the top of the path and looked back at Pirate and the other seal, still playing with the Frisbee. Slowly it dawned on him that the female was probably Pirate's mate. He smiled to himself at the thought that he now had two seals in his life. A breeze had begun to whip the waves into little white-capped furrows and it blew into Ryan's wet shirt, making it cling to him in cold, damp patches. He shivered and increased his pace towards the cottage; he couldn't wait to tell his father the good news.

Matthew sprang to his feet the instant he saw Ryan burst through the door, wet, bedraggled but grinning from ear to ear. "Guess what's happened, Dad?"

Matthew eyed his son cautiously but smiled as he replied, "You went swimming with all your clothes on?"

"*We* went swimming, Dad. *We!* Me and *Pirate.* He's back! And he's got a mate!"

At first Matthew thought Ryan was mistaken. But when he looked at his son's face, he knew there could be no mistake – Ryan couldn't confuse Pirate with another seal. The amazing news of Pirate's return made Matthew's happiness complete. He had changed so much since the shock of almost losing Ryan.

A warm bath followed by hot soup and bed awaited Ryan once he eventually stopped recounting how he and Pirate had been re-united in the cove. Deliriously happy, he closed his eyes that night with a vision of the two seals playing in the waves. But into his dreams crept images from another night when Ryan had seen Pirate leading a little band of seals towards the cove, struggling against the stormy waters, made even more hazardous by the thick, choking oil. When Ryan woke the next morning, he was relieved to find it was just a dream – Pirate was home again and probably waiting for a game in the cove that very moment.

Chapter 11

Pirate often appeared in the cove with his mate, and Ryan was nearly always there to greet them with little gifts: some fresh mackerel, a ball, and a new Frisbee. They enjoyed the presents but Pirate always swam off with the old Frisbee when they left the cove. The seals made a beautiful sight, whether engaged in an energetic game of chase, or a gentle glide like two dancers waltzing along the surface of the water. When the female failed to accompany Pirate on several, successive days, Ryan became concerned. But Pirate didn't seem at all distressed, so Ryan felt reassured that all was probably well.

The warm evenings brought the two friends together again as they resumed the pleasure of basking in the last rays of the sun at the edge of the water. Looking into the seal's black, watery eyes, Ryan wondered what secrets they held of places deep below the waves, where creatures battled to survive by using their strength or cunning. The seal's intelligent eyes always stared back at Ryan, revealing nothing. Generations of seals had taught their young how to survive and passed on their skills to help them. Throughout bitter weather, shortage of food, disease and all the challenges that Nature and man had thrown at them, the amazing creatures had survived. Behind Pirate's comical expression lay a mind as sharp as the fishermen's hooks he had learned to avoid.

Ryan woke up earlier than usual the next morning. At the bottom of his bed he noticed a large brown paper parcel. As it was addressed to him, he hurriedly tore into it. Inside was a complete school uniform with a badge of gold, green and red shining impressively on the blazer pocket. Having tried it on, he hardly recognized himself. As he stared at the reflection of a stranger in the mirror, he felt confused. Was this what he wanted? Did he really want to leave behind the freedom of the island and Pirate, or to be parted from his father now that he had just found him again? He felt sure his father would provide for a tutor to visit the island if he chose to stay, rather than go to the big school.

Ryan stared and stared into the mirror, searching for an answer. Eventually it came to him. If he turned down the opportunity of the school and all it had to offer him, he might regret it in the future. He knew his father was delighted he had gained a place at such an excellent school, and was keen for him to attend it. Ryan thought about Pirate and realized that the seal's life was changing too. He had moved on to adulthood. Ryan knew that school work would offer him a challenge and the company of others of his age; he needed that if he was to grow. It had been arranged for him to board with a family whose son was to attend the school. Ryan knew he had to try it at least. He could always return at weekends and of course there were the long holidays. He would work hard at school and look forward all the more to the times he would spend with Pirate and his father.

It was with mixed feelings that Ryan headed for the cove for a last encounter with Pirate before leaving the island to start at the new school. He stood at the edge of the water, idly throwing pebbles to the waves, which caught them but didn't return them. Soon the familiar head with its jaunty black eye patch popped up from the water. Pirate did not move; there were no barks of pleasure to announce his arrival. Cautiously the seal moved nearer to Ryan, who was puzzled by the animal's behaviour. He stayed perfectly still while Pirate began to cruise along the surface of the water a little way out from the shore. He stared at Ryan as though seeing him for the first time. Dressed in school uniform, Ryan looked a very different creature from the one Pirate usually saw. "Don't

be afraid, Pirate! It's still *me* inside these clothes."

He laughed and then became silent. There was an uneasiness and sadness between them. Pirate stayed perfectly still. Ryan broke the silence.

"I've come to say goodbye for a while – but not for ever. I'll keep coming back to see you – I promise!"

Ryan took a deep breath as he continued bravely, "Look after everyone for me. I know they'll be safe with you around."

Pirate appeared to understand every word. The old Frisbee floated alongside him as usual, but he made no attempt to play. Slowly he moved out of the water and waddled up to Ryan, who bent down to stroke the seal's silky head lovingly. Just for a moment, Pirate looked up, his big, black watery eyes focusing on his friend, then he backed into the water, retrieved the Frisbee, and sank below. Ryan stood up and waited – but Pirate did not reappear.

Chapter 12

Ryan boarded the helicopter with an air of self confidence, partly for the benefit of his father. He wanted him to feel proud of his son. So much had changed between them, that it was difficult for Ryan to recall the way they had existed before the night of the storm. As the weeks passed, Matthew had enjoyed life more and more, taking an active part in the little island's social life; no longer the tall, silent man who lived in Lighthouse Cottage.

Ryan remembered the times he had wanted nothing better than to live on the mainland – now it was only a short flight away. Since those times, he had learned that happiness could be found in the people around him, and that if it wasn't to be found, it could be made. One misty morning he had chanced upon a seal in the cove, alone like him, and, with that same spirit of adventure about him. Together, they had created their own happiness. Did he really want to trade evenings in the surf with Pirate, for a classroom full of children? Doubt nagged at Ryan once again.

Just before he had boarded the helicopter, his father had hugged him and handed him a brand new pair of binoculars. "If ever you feel a little homesick, just point these towards the island. They're powerful, but I doubt if you'll see me or Pirate. But remember, as long as you can see the lighthouse beam, you'll know that we're there."

As the helicopter rose from the ground Ryan waved to his father, Miss Roberts and the little band of well-wishers who had gathered to see him off. Already the island looked smaller. Slowly they moved out over the sea, the whirring blades causing the water to fan out in great ripples. His father and the others were still waving to him. Ryan gave them a last wave back then settled in his seat to enjoy the crossing.

They had just passed the very tip of the island, and coming into view were a group of rocks. Ryan recalled how much he had always wanted to visit them but his father refused to take him as the currents surrounding them were very hazardous. It was rumoured that several shipwrecks lay deep on the seabed at their base, the fate of the crews sealed with them, leaving only legends and handed-down stories as a warning to all who approached the rocks. Ryan smiled as he remembered how the old islanders excited the children with tales of secret caves hidden within them. Smugglers too, were reputed to have used them for storing hoards of rum, brandy and fine wines. The old ones of the island delighted in telling of others who had used the rocks' secret caverns, hiding themselves from capture by the authorities. These were the boldest adventurers of all – daring robbers of the sea lanes, capable of surviving treacherous seas and cold, stormy weather ... pirates!

Hardly had the word entered Ryan's head when, looking down, he saw two seals on the rocks. One was in the water at the edge of the rocks, and the other was lying on a ledge close to the waves. Great rollers lashed at the little rocky fortress. The helicopter banked, moving closer to the rocks for a moment as it positioned itself on course for the mainland. Ryan needed a much closer look at the seals. Delighted, he remembered his father's parting gift and reached down for his new binoculars. Focusing carefully, he gained a much clearer view. The one on the rocks looked remarkably like Pirate's mate, while the one in the water, as he frolicked in the foaming surf with an old Frisbee in his mouth, was unmistakably familiar. The black mark in the shape of a pirate's patch over one eye stated his identity beyond doubt. There, reflected Ryan, smiling to himself, was a true pirate of the high seas!

Had the amazing creature survived the storm and the sickening oil slick by hiding within the protection of the rocky fortress, like the pirates of days gone by? If so, how had he got there on that terrible night? Could the great waves have swept him there? Even so, how had he healed and cleaned himself, fed and recovered, when he must have been just as badly affected as so many other seals in need of attention? Pirate had even found himself a mate to share his kingdom.

Not even Ryan would ever know the full story of Pirate's survival and return. It was all part of the seal's mystery – the incredible creature he had come to know.

Pirate looked up at the helicopter as its blades whirred high above him. Through his binoculars, Ryan saw him hurl the old Frisbee into the air and, for a moment, he wondered whether the seal knew in his uncanny way that his friend was watching. Ryan wished he could reach out and catch the Frisbee just one more time.

Suddenly Ryan's eyes were diverted from

Pirate to a seal pup who had dashed from the safety of his mother's side to throw himself into the frothing waves. With incredible skill and accuracy, the little creature swam to where the Frisbee was about to land and caught it in his mouth before it fell. Battling his way back through the heavy surf, he reached his mother who anxiously awaited his safe return.

Ryan hurriedly adjusted his binoculars again, this time to focus on the pup, before he disappeared out of range. In the last precious second, as the helicopter gathered speed, he saw all he had wanted to know. The valiant little seal was covered in fluffy, cream fur, apart from around one eye, where there was an unmistakable black mark – like a pirate's patch.

If you like animals, then you'll love
Hippo Animal Stories!

Thunderfoot
Deborah van der Beek
When Mel finds the enormous, neglected horse Thunderfoot, she doesn't know it will change her life for ever...

Vanilla Fudge
Deborah van der Beek
When Lizzie and Hannah fall in love with the same dog, neither of them will give up without a fight...

A Foxcub Named Freedom
Brenda Jobling
An injured vixen nudges her young son away from her. She can sense danger and cares nothing for herself – only for her son's freedom...

Midnight Dancer
Midnight Dancer 2: To Catch a Thief
Midnight Dancer 3: Running Free
Midnight Dancer 4: Fireraisers
Elizabeth Lindsay
Follow the adventures of Mory and her pony, Midnight Dancer.

Animal Rescue
Bette Paul
Can Tessa help save the badgers of Delves Wood from destruction?

HIPPO FANTASY

Lose yourself in a whole new world, a world where anything is possible – from wizards and dragons, to time travel and new civilizations... Gripping, thrilling, scary and funny by turns, these Hippo Fantasy titles will hold you captivated to the very last page.

The Night of Wishes
Michael Ende

Malcolm and the Cloud-Stealer
Douglas Hill

The Crystal Keeper
James Jauncey

The Wednesday Wizard
Sherryl Jordan

Ratspell
Paddy Mounter

Rowan of Rin
Rowan and the Travellers
Emily Rodda

The Practical Princess
Jay Williams

R.L.Stine

Reader beware, you're in for a scare!
These terrifying tales will send shivers up your spine:

1 **Welcome to Dead House**
2 **Say Cheese and Die!**
3 **Stay out of the Basement**
4 **The Curse of the Mummy's Tomb**
5 **Monster Blood**
6 **Let's Get Invisible**
7 **Night of the Living Dummy**
8 **The Girl Who Cried Monster**
9 **Welcome to Camp Nightmare**
10 **The Ghost Next Door**
11 **The Haunted Mask**
12 **Piano Lessons Can Be Murder**
13 **Be Careful What You Wish For**
14 **The Werewolf of Fever Swamp**
15 **You Can't Scare Me**
16 **One Day at Horrorland**
17 **Why I'm Afraid of Bees**
18 **Monster Blood II**
19 **Deep Trouble**
20 **Go Eat Worms**
21 **Return of the Mummy**
22 **The Scarecrow Walks at Midnight**
23 **Attack of the Mutant**
24 **My Hairiest Adventure**
25 **A Night in Terror Tower**
26 **The Cuckoo Clock of Doom**
27 **Monster Blood III**
28 **Ghost Beach**
29 **Phantom of the Auditorium**
30 **It Came From Beneath the Sink!**

Need a babysitter? Then call the Babysitters Club. Kristy Thomas and her friends are all experienced sitters. They can tackle any job from rampaging toddlers to a pandemonium of pets. To find out all about them, read on!

1. **Kristy's Great Idea**
2. **Claudia and the Phantom Phone Calls**
3. **The Truth About Stacey**
4. **Mary Anne Saves The Day**
5. **Dawn and the Impossible Three**
6. **Kristy's Big Day**
7. **Claudia and Mean Janine**
8. **Boy-Crazy Stacey**
9. **The Ghost At Dawn's House**
10. **Logan Likes Mary Anne!**
11. **Kristy and the Snobs**
12. **Claudia and the New Girl**
13. **Goodbye Stacey, Goodbye**
14. **Hello, Mallory**
15. **Little Miss Stoneybrook ... and Dawn**
16. **Jessi's Secret Language**
17. **Mary Anne's Bad-Luck Mystery**
18. **Stacey's Mistake**
19. **Claudia and the Bad Joke**
20. **Kristy and the Walking Disaster**
21. **Mallory and the Trouble With Twins**
22. **Jessi Ramsey, Pet-Sitter**
23. **Dawn On The Coast**
24. **Kristy and the Mother's Day Surprise**
25. **Mary Anne and the Search For Tigger**
26. **Claudia and the Sad Goodbye**
27. **Jessi and the Superbrat**
28. **Welcome Back, Stacey!**
29. **Mallory and the Mystery Diary**
30. **Mary Anne and the Great Romance**
31. **Dawn's Wicked Stepsister**

32. Kristy and the Secret Of Susan
33. Claudia and the Great Search
34. Mary Anne and Too Many Boys
35. Stacey and the Mystery Of Stoneybrook
36. Jessi's Babysitter
37. Dawn and the Older Boy
38. Kristy's Mystery Admirer
39. Poor Mallory!
40. Claudia and the Middle School Mystery
41. Mary Anne Vs. Logan
42. Jessi and the Dance School Phantom
43. Stacey's Emergency
44. Dawn and the Big Sleepover
45. Kristy and the Baby Parade
46. Mary Anne Misses Logan
47. Mallory On Strike
48. Jessi's Wish
49. Claudia and the Genius Of Elm Street
50. Dawn's Big Date
51. Stacey's Ex-Best Friend
52. Mary Anne and Too Many Babies
53. Kristy For President
54. Mallory and the Dream Horse
55. Jessi's Gold Medal
56. Keep Out, Claudia!
57. Dawn Saves The Planet
58. Stacey's Choice
59. Mallory Hates Boys (and Gym)
60. Mary Anne's Makeover
61. Jessi and the Awful Secret
62. Kristy and the Worst Kid Ever
63. Claudia's ~~Freind~~ Friend
64. Dawn's Family Feud
65. Stacey's Big Crush
66. Maid Mary Anne
67. Dawn's Big Move
68. Jessi and the Bad Babysitter
69. Get Well Soon, Mallory!
70. Stacey and the Cheerleaders
71. Claudia and the Perfect Boy
72. Dawn and the We Love Kids Club
73. Mary Anne and Miss Priss
74. Kristy and the Copycat